Keela found herself standing in a small cell, much like the one she had left behind, except this one was darker, for the sun had set. Moonlight filtered through the narrow window high overhead, cloaking the room in velvet shadows.

Great, thought Keela. Some escape route. What idiot made a tunnel to nowhere?

There was nothing to do but search the room. She ran her hands over the walls, looking for signs of a secret passage, for any kind of hope. In the corner, her hands discovered something soft and hairy slumped upon the floor—and that something was alive!

———————
————————————

BOOKS

by

Michael Andrews

The Wizard's Tale

The Thief's Tale

The Warrior's Tale

The Elf's Tale

The Thief's Tale

Michael Andrews

TSR Inc.™

For Dixie, Troy, and Beth, who have given me
treasures beyond compare.

—A.H.

THE THIEF'S TALE

First Printing: November 1993
Printed in the United States of America
Library of Congress Catalog Card Number: 93-60923

9 8 7 6 5 4 3 2 1

ISBN: 1-56076-897-5

TSR, Inc.
P.O. Box 756
Lake Geneva, WI 53147
United States of America

TSR Ltd.
120 Church End, Cherry Hinton
Cambridge CB1 3LB
United Kingdom

Chapter One

The day dawned like any other in Keela's fifteen years: she was hungry. If this were a typical morning, she might haunt a cottage window, waiting for a pie to be set out to cool, or raid a chicken coop. Or, after hastily smoothing her gold-and-copper curls, she might convince the baker's apprentice to offer her a bit of cake.

But this was the week of Lord Rufus's sixteenth birthday, and his mother, Baroness Von Drek, had arranged an impressive celebration. The entire village of Durham had turned out to see traveling

1

entertainers and take part in contests of skill. The festivity made it easy for Keela to slink through the milling crowd and "liberate" a snack without being noticed. She was munching on a wedge of sourdough bread when she spotted *him*—the boy.

He was tall and sturdy, and quite handsome beneath the thin layer of dust that shrouded him. She pegged the fair-haired lad for a shepherd, or perhaps a woodcutter. His eyes were large and dark, his jaw was strong, and his face was tanned and smooth. By the lambskin cloak swung round his shoulders, she also guessed that he, like Keela herself, was spending his nights alone beneath the stars, out in the cold.

But it was not his good looks that captured Keela's attention. The boy had entered a contest of strength, along with a half dozen youths from the village. Each was to heft a rock the size of a man's head. The one who threw it the farthest won a fat quail, fit for a peasant's supper.

When it came time for the newcomer to throw, he displayed a unique style, spinning like a top before he let the stone fly. Keela didn't see the rock as it soared through the air. In fact, she barely noticed the boy's skillful technique. For as he spun round, a brilliant flash of gold caught her eye. And no mere rock—unless it was a gem, of course—

could interest her as much as something so beautiful.

The effort of throwing caused the boy's tunic to fall open, revealing an amulet that hung round his neck. For just a moment, the amulet shone brightly in the morning sun. Keela could make out the delicate swirl of precious metals, forming a knot around a deep blue stone. She had seen such fine craftsmanship only once before, but once was enough. She knew this was the magical work of woodland elves.

The rock hit the ground with a dull thud, raising a small cloud of dust. It outdistanced every other stone by several yards.

"The lad must have giants' blood in 'im!" exclaimed an onlooker, and his companions clapped in approval.

The boy righted himself, then tucked the amulet back into his tunic. As far as Keela could tell, only she had noticed its shining beauty.

What kind of shepherd owns a thing of such value? she thought as she watched him step forward to claim his prize. Surely, he must have stolen the amulet. And since *he* was not its rightful owner, then he couldn't complain if someone—a clever girl, perhaps—relieved him of this burden. She might even discover to whom the amulet belonged and return it for a reward. Of course, it could take years to track that person down. . . .

The boy tucked the quail's wooden cage beneath his arm and headed into the crowd. Keela followed, waiting for a chance to approach him unnoticed. The boy soon paused to watch a juggler, and the thief moved closer.

That's it . . . Keela thought. Just keep your eye on the balls. . . .

Then she spotted the guard. A seven-foot-tall brute was parting the crowd to her right. He looked like an ogre crashing through a henhouse. In fact, given his size and his dark, heavy brow, Keela guessed that an ogre *had* invaded a distant branch of his family tree (though to mention it, of course, would be quite an insult).

The guard wore a chain-mail shirt, and a huge broadsword hung at his side. The shirt was topped by a tabard displaying the black-and-purple heraldry of the duke, who ruled all the lands within a day's ride. Rufus Von Drek, the birthday boy, was Duke Edward's nephew.

"Blast," Keela muttered, still eyeing the guard. "It was only a loaf of bread. Who could've fingered me?"

But the guard paid her no heed. Instead, he veered straight toward the lad and shouted, "You there, with the quail!"

The boy turned to see who had addressed him. A look of fear washed over his face. He leaped away, dropping the quail and stumbling as he fled.

"So you *are* a thief," Keela said softly. "And a flat-footed one at that."

The guard was fast closing in on the boy. Keela stood near enough to intersect the big man's path. In one smooth gesture, the agile girl drew a bullwhip from the sash at her waist. Keela's mother, also a thief, had left her daughter two things when she had died five years ago: the whip and an independent spirit. So far, both had served Keela well.

As the guard passed, Keela lashed out at the ground, deftly snagging his ankle. The guard crashed into the dirt. When he turned to face his attacker, she was just a flash of reddish gold hair, disappearing into the distance. The boy, too, seemed to have vanished, but not to the watchful eyes of a clever female rogue. . . .

It took a bit of work, but Keela soon picked up the shepherd's trail in the woods. Once she found the signs, they weren't difficult to follow—a fresh footprint here, a scrap of clothing there, and no shortage of broken twigs. He had shown some smarts when he had reached a narrow stream, however. There, the trail ran cold.

Keela leaped to a smooth gray rock in the middle

of the brook. Her blue eyes scanned the scene, hungry for any sign of her quarry, no matter how small. The mud on the opposite bank held no print to betray him. Keela listened, but heard only the gentle rushing of the water, and a jay's raucous call upstream. Playing a hunch, Keela stepped into the water and followed the bird's sound.

After several minutes, she again saw the trail beside the bank. By the depth of his footprints, Keela knew that the boy had stopped running. He was walking along the stream, weaving in and out of the forest wherever the lush foliage hugged the water's edge, and crossing the brook wherever an occasional tree lay across it.

Keela followed his meandering trail for more than an hour. She knew the woods well and suspected where he might pause for a break. When the thief glimpsed him ahead, she knew she was right. The boy had reached the brook's source, an isolated woodland pool. Keela crept silently toward a nearby tree and climbed it to get a better look.

The pool was surrounded by willows. Their low, draping branches formed a curtain at the water's edge. At the far side, a spring bubbled from an outcropping of granite, creating a tiny waterfall that fed the pool. Birds flitted past, chattering at the boy's intrusion into their paradise.

Unaware of his audience, the boy seated himself on a mossy bank. He removed his worn leather boots, then plunged his soiled feet into the clear water. With a sigh of exhaustion, he watched the dirt drift slowly toward the pool's sandy bottom. He rolled up his trouser legs and massaged his calves. Then he waded in to survey the scene.

By all appearances, he was alone. He returned to the mossy bank and began to remove the rest of his tattered clothing, pausing to carefully fold each item.

"Get on with it, lad," Keela muttered softly. "It feels like I've been in this tree for hours."

His well-muscled back was turned, but she could still glimpse the golden chain shining against his smooth skin, just below the waves of his hair. She didn't care whether he swam buck naked or dived in fully dressed. She just wanted him to remove the amulet. For a moment, she feared he would take off every item *except* that. Then, at last, she saw him lift something over his head. It had to be the amulet— he had nothing else left to remove.

The boy knelt, tucked the object into his clothing, then dived into the pool. He resurfaced in the middle. After another quick look around and a toss of his wet hair, he turned and swam toward the rocks on the opposite side.

Keela seized her chance. She dropped from the

tree and sneaked toward the clothing. Then she knelt beside it and began to search the folds.

"Hey!" the boy shouted.

Keela looked up.

"Get your thieving hands off my clothes, girl," yelled the boy, "or I'll take 'em off for you!" He was swimming quickly toward her. In three strong strokes, he regained his footing and started to rise from the water.

"Oh, I believe you, good sir," Keela said sweetly, dropping the clothes to the ground. "I can see you've taken off quite a lot already!"

The boy blushed and stopped cold, waist high in the water. Keela kept talking, trying to keep him off guard.

"Besides," she said coyly, "I didn't see you there at first. And if you don't stop right where you are, I'll have a look at more than I care to!" She put a hand to her brow as if to avert her eyes, though she clearly continued to peek.

"Sorry," the boy replied, stammering self-consciously. "Just step away from my belongings."

Keela winked. "Not a chance, lad," she said.

With that, the nimble thief snatched up the entire bundle of clothes, boots and all. "Catch me if you can!" she shouted over her shoulder. "But watch out for those brambles!" In a flash, she was gone.

It wasn't difficult to elude her pursuer. Keela moved like a panther—quiet and swift. Her slim leggings and short tunic allowed her to leap and climb with ease.

When she was sure she hadn't been followed, the thief doubled back and headed to her favorite spot in the forest. A short journey from the pool stood a towering oak. Its roots spread over the ground like the tentacles of a giant squid, amid a sea of emerald-green moss. Keela knew the boy was unlikely to find her. The forest was dense, and its overgrown paths formed a confusing maze. She sat beneath the oak and began to search through the shepherd's belongings.

First, she emptied a small leather pouch, which held a few shillings and little else. The boy's tunic yielded nothing; it didn't even have a hidden pocket. Keela rifled his trousers and cape. Again, nothing. She peered into a boot, then turned it upside down. An amulet fell out—but it was not the one she sought. Instead, this was a cheap piece of lead and glass, bearing no resemblance to the dazzling piece she had seen round the boy's neck. Angrily she tossed the worthless necklace to the ground and searched the other boot. Nothing.

A crow flew to the tree and began to caw, as if to laugh at the thief's predicament.

"You don't have to rub it in," she answered. "I know I lost the darned thing." That was the only explanation. In her hasty escape, she must have dropped the golden amulet in the forest. Or, worse yet, what if she had lost it at the onset, when gathering up the clothes?

"Well, Keela," she said, "you'll just have to hope that isn't so."

She began to retrace her path through the forest, scanning the ground as she went. It seemed hopeless. She traveled all the way back to the pool, but still she found nothing—not even the boy.

Unfortunately, someone found *her*. When Keela turned to retrace her steps yet again, she came face-to-chest with a guardsman—the one she had felled like a tree in the village. He didn't look happy to see her.

The enormous man seized the girl by her slender shoulders, pinning her arms to her sides. Her feet dangled above the ground.

"Well, well," grumbled the brute. "Looks like I've caught me a jackrabbit."

"Oh, sir!" Keela gushed, batting her heavy lashes. "I'm so glad you've come along. I fear I'm lost and—"

"Don't waste yer breath," the guardsman interrupted. "I recognize that mop of yours. And if I'm not mistaken, that's a whip hanging from your sash."

Keela squirmed, but his grip held fast.

The guard laughed. "You're short, but you're feisty," he said. "How 'bout you and I make a trip to the dungeon? We got something that'll help make you taller." He lifted her up to his face and grinned, revealing a row of badly stained teeth.

Keela smiled back. Then she bit him hard on the nose. He yelled and loosened his grip. For a split second, she slipped toward the earth. Then the guard seized her neck. Now Keela's arms were free. Gasping for breath, the thief reached up and grabbed her captor's little finger. She twisted it sharply backward and heard the bone snap like a twig. Her captor yowled and let go. Keela landed in a heap.

She scrambled to her feet and started to run. Unfortunately, the guard ran after her, cussing and roaring all the while. Even worse for Keela, he was fast. Twice he managed to snatch a piece of her tunic, but each time she narrowly escaped. Three times they raced round the same tree, dodging and weaving, then changing direction. Finally, Keela outdistanced him. She charged ahead, entering an unfamiliar part of the woods. Then she pulled up short. She had come to the edge of a deep ravine. Panting, the guard approached from behind.

"What's your hurry, miss?" he growled. "Our lit-

A scene from the DRAGON STRIKE™ video

little party has just begun."

Keela took the bullwhip from her belt and lashed out at his feet. He sidestepped, and the whip missed him by a yard.

"You didn't think I'd fall for that twice, did you?" said the guard with a sneer.

"A girl can hope," Keela replied. She flashed her whip again, this time over the man's head. The whip found its mark. A dead branch crashed onto his shoulders, knocking the guard into the ravine.

Keela stepped to the edge to admire her handiwork. "Gee," she said. "Looks like you fell for it after all."

Battered and moaning, the guard lay at the bottom of the slope in a pile of leaves. Keela barely heard the sudden rustle behind her, but she felt the blow. Something hard smashed against the back of her skull. The thief pitched forward, thrashing blindly, then tumbled head over heels, again and again, until the scene whirling past her faded into darkness.

Chapter Two

The world was black, and Keela's head throbbed. She pictured a team of dwarven miners inside it, swinging sledgehammers against a rock wall. Then the wall began to crumble, and Keela heard the sound of blood rushing past her ears. She struggled to open her eyes.

"Poor, dear girl . . ." said a woman's voice. The words oozed through the din like molasses. Someone was stroking Keela's cheek, but there was nothing comforting about the touch.

"Poor, poor little bird . . ."

The thief's eyes fluttered open. Just inches from her face, a blood-red snake was wriggling upon a field of white. Then the snake split into two, and a row of teeth appeared. The thief jerked herself away, smashing her head against a stone wall. *This* wall was real. Keela's pain intensified.

A man chortled in the background.

"Shut up, Titus!" snapped the woman. Then her voice regained its honeyed tone. "It's time to wake up, little mouse. That's right . . . ."

Keela's vision cleared. Before her loomed the face of a middle-aged woman. The two red snakes became a pair of lips, impossibly thin and stretched. They were drawn into a crooked smile, which twitched ever so slightly at the corners. The white field broadened into skin, which was wrinkled and heavily powdered.

"I imagine our guest would like some water," cooed the woman. Her tone was hardly sincere. "Give me the flask, Titus."

Behind her stood two men. The first was massive. Keela recognized the dark-haired guard from the forest. His broad, flat nose was bandaged, and so was one of his fingers. The other man, closer to the door, was thin and slight of build. He swayed to and fro like a nervous animal. When he felt Keela's gaze on him, he met it and grinned, drawing a sleeve across his runny nose. His nostrils twitched, and his beady eyes sparkled. At his side hung a blood-stained club—the source of Keela's headache, no doubt.

"How rude of me," said the woman. "Allow me to introduce myself. I am Baroness Von Drek."

Keela had already guessed this was someone important. But the thief hadn't figured on meeting the most powerful woman in the duchy! Baroness Von Drek was Duke Edward's sister. The duke was a widower, and everyone knew he relied on his sister for advice.

The baroness was clad in a purple gown made of rustling silk. Yards of black lace covered the arms and skirt, hanging from the dress like glistening cobwebs. A high, stiff collar framed the woman's face, which was anything but pleasant. Her features were sharp and shrewish, and her eyes were cold and gray. Her jet-black hair was piled high, with two white streaks at the temples. The heavy white powder made her teeth look yellow by comparison. The only color against the white skin was the dark red of her lips, which writhed like separate animals, as if they had been mired in the powder and could not escape.

The baroness pointed to the husky man with a bandaged face. He handed her a leather flask.

"You've already met Titus, of course," said the woman to Keela. "The other fellow is Darg." The weasel-faced man flashed his sharp little teeth. "Darg is a bit of the silent type," continued the baroness. "But, then, you already know how silent he can be." She pressed the flask to Keela's lips, and the thief drank the water gratefully.

"Now, isn't that better?" asked the baroness, returning the flask to Titus. "Are you comfortable, dear?" she asked.

Of course Keela was not. She was chained to the wall, with her arms bound overhead. Both feet were manacled together. Her head continued to pound. Moreover, every muscle in her body ached, and the manacles bit into her wrists.

"You could loosen these chains," Keela replied.

"Why, yes, I suppose I could," said the baroness dryly. "But first, you'll have to do something for *me*. . . ."

Keela answered in the sweetest tone possible. "Certainly, Your Ladyship, though I cannot imagine what an unimportant orphan like me could possibly do for someone of your position. . . ."

"What, indeed," replied the baroness sharply, extending a clawlike hand toward Keela's face. She spread the fingers slowly for effect, unfolding one after another as if she were opening a fan. Each white, bony digit ended in a long red nail, curled slightly at the tip. The baroness began to stroke her forefinger across Keela's cheek.

"It would seem, dear girl, that you have put your nose where it doesn't belong." She tapped Keela's nose to emphasize the point. "Titus knows the unfortunate result of such actions, don't you, Titus?"

The man with the bandaged face only sneered, for he knew no response was expected.

"But for now," the baroness continued, "I am interested in your eyes, and what they have seen. You must tell me what happened to the boy and his amulet." The baroness traced a path around Keela's right eye with her fingernail, bringing it to rest upon the girl's temple.

"What boy? What amulet?" the thief asked with innocence.

"Don't toy with me," hissed the baroness, digging her nail into Keela's skin. "Titus tells me you couldn't take your pretty eyes off that shepherd in the village. The boy wore an amulet resembling one that was stolen from me years ago. If you hadn't interfered, I would have it back already. Now, someone must be punished for this wrong. The question remains, dear, will that someone be *you* . . . ?"

Keela didn't answer. The baroness pressed harder, and the thief felt a trickle of blood running down her face.

"Honest, I don't know what you're talking about!" Keela cried.

The baroness raised her hand as if to strike. Instinctively, Keela shut her eyes, but the expected blow never came. Instead, the baroness merely laughed, then strode toward the cell's heavy oak door. Her skirts rustled and hissed as she moved. Titus pulled the door open. The baroness turned toward Keela.

"Poor girl," she said, in a low and throaty voice. "That bump on your head must have clouded your memory. Perhaps a good night's sleep will help you remember where the amulet lies."

"I'll try my best to please you, milady," replied Keela.

"Oh, I'm sure you will," said the baroness. She curled her lips in a wicked half-smile. "For if you do not, I will simply torture you to death."

With that, she turned and left. The little man called Darg scurried after her. Titus pulled the door shut, and Keela heard him slide the heavy bolt into place on the opposite side. Then a tiny window in the door swung open. Through the bars Keela could barely make out Titus's heavy black brows and his white, bandaged nose.

"Pleasant dreams," he snarled. "See you in the

morning."

Keela waited until he had closed the little portal and she heard his footsteps echoing in the corridor. Then she let out her breath. "Don't count on it," she whispered.

The thief scanned her prison. Escape would be difficult, but Keela was small, and she had escaped from shackles twice before. This time, her life depended on it.

She ran her feet over the earthen floor beneath her, gathering up mud. Then she drew herself into a ball and rubbed her muddy feet over her left hand to make it slick. Keela struggled to pull the hand free. Still no luck. The thief took aim and spat at her hand. She pulled again. Tears welled in her eyes, and her hand began to bleed. Then, at last, she was free—at least in part.

She reached into the hem of her tunic and withdrew a small pin, the kind designed for picking locks. Using her free hand, she inserted the pick into the manacle that bound her other wrist, then jiggled until she heard the telltale click. The manacle came open, and the thief collapsed to the floor. She used the pick to remove the iron bonds at her feet. The first part of her escape was over, but Keela knew the hardest part was still to come.

The door was barred and bolted from the outside, making her lockpick utterly useless against it. No hinges were exposed, but she had no tools for breaking them anyway. A tiny barred window lay high overhead in the wall. Keela scaled the wall to reach it—only to find that the bars held fast, and the opening was far too narrow to crawl through.

She dropped to the floor, discouraged. Her head ached, and her left hand still bled, despite the wrapping she had made from a scrap of her tunic.

As if to add insult to injury, a rat scurried into the room. Keela hated all vermin, but she despised rats most of all. Rats carried the Fever, and the Fever had taken her mother. Still, she had to admire the creatures, if for nothing else but their ability to flatten their disgustingly filthy bodies into a fraction of their normal size. The crack under the door was barely visible, but the rat had managed to sneak through.

Or had it?

Keela gathered a handful of mud from the floor and threw it at the rodent. It squealed at her defiantly, then slipped into the shadowy corner of the room. Keela followed. The rat was gone.

"Where did you go, you little dung-monger?" the thief whispered softly, running her hand over the stones in the corner of her cell. Then she found it—a narrow crevice at the base of the wall. Cursing herself for not finding it sooner, she began to pick at the mud. The crack grew wider. After an hour's work, the stone was loose.

Keela held her breath. "Could I be this lucky?" she asked, tugging on the stone with all her might. It gave way, revealing a tunnel about knee-high. A thousand sow bugs swarmed into the cell. "Maybe not so lucky," Keela muttered as she knelt and wriggled inside, crunching the insects with her hands and knees.

The tunnel was damp and pitch black. It quickly turned and narrowed, and Keela had to drag herself along on her stomach. Something small and cold crawled under her tunic, but she forced herself to ignore it.

It could be worse, she thought. She knew that tunnels could be home to oozing slimes that ate through metal, and worms that dropped from the ceiling to chew their way into your brain. Keela told herself she had only normal vermin for company, and she hoped it was true. The thief knew one thing for sure—whatever lay ahead in the tunnel was no worse than her fate at the hands of the baroness.

Then the tunnel came to an end. Keela pushed against the wall, and a rock gave way. She heard it thud to the ground a few feet below. There was nothing to do but follow.

She found herself standing in a small cell, much

like the one she had left behind, except this one was darker, for the sun had set. Moonlight filtered in through the narrow window high overhead, cloaking the room in velvet shadows.

Great, thought Keela. Some escape route. What idiot made a tunnel to nowhere?

There was nothing to do but search the room. She ran her hands over the walls, looking for signs of a secret passage, for any kind of hope. In the corner, her hands discovered something soft and hairy slumped upon the floor—and that something was alive!

Chapter Three

Who's there?" rasped the creature in the corner.

Keela leaped backward. "I'm a . . . a friend," she stammered, trying desperately to make out the speaker's contours.

The creature cackled in reply, then sighed deeply. "That remains to be seen," it whispered.

"Oh, but I am a friend!" said the thief, taking another step backward. "And I won't hurt you if you promise me the same. I'm just a poor peasant girl, wrongly sent to these dungeons."

"You're no ordinary peasant girl," said the voice

A scene from the DRAGON STRIKE™ video

hoarsely, "or you would not have made it to this cell."

Keela's eyes began to make out the source of the voice. She saw a hunchbacked figure crouched in the corner. A tangled mass of filthy gray hair covered its face and cloaked its shoulders. Then the figure extended a ghostly white hand and searched the air, as if trying to touch the visitor.

Keela sighed in relief. The creature was an old, crippled woman. "Tell me your name, girl," said the voice.

"Keela," the thief replied. "And yours?"

The old woman sighed. "I don't recall it at the moment, but that doesn't matter." She patted the ground beside her. "Sit beside me and tell me how you came to this cell. It's been a long time since I've heard a good story. And, mind you, tell me the truth. I may be blind, but I can see through your lies."

Keela looked at the moonlight shining faintly in the window overhead. "I haven't much time," she said. "If they find me here in the morning, I'll be dead."

"Do not worry, child. I'll help you escape. But first, you must grant me your company."

"How could *you* help me escape?" Keela protested.

"Just as I helped the previous inhabitant of your

cell escape, over ten years ago."

"If that's so, why are you still here yourself?"

"I'm growing weary of your questions, child," the woman replied. "Can you not see I am old and blind? Where you will soon go, I cannot follow. But first, you must sit down beside me." She patted the ground again.

Keela eyed her companion nervously. What if this was a trick?

The woman cackled softly. "Are you afraid of a crippled old hag?" she asked, as if she had read the thief's thoughts.

Reluctantly, Keela sat down beside her. The woman reached out to touch her face. The hand was filthy, and it smelled of decay, but Keela resisted the urge to retch.

"Such a pretty face," said the hag. "And a good heart. I can sense that, too."

The hag leaned closer and smiled, revealing her toothless gums. Her breath was foul. A clump of straw poked out from the gray, tangled mass of hair, and Keela tentatively reached out to free it. The thief shrank back in surprise. She had expected to find two milky, unseeing eyes, but instead the woman had no eyes at all—just two empty, shriveled pits where her eyes should have been.

"The baroness put them out," replied the woman

to Keela's unspoken question. "So you see, Arakeela of Dragonwyk, I, too, am personally acquainted with the lady of this castle."

Keela gasped and sprang to her feet. "How did you know my full name," she asked, "when you claim that you don't even know your own? Are you a witch?"

"I simply know, and it is not for you or me to understand. Now, it is important that you tell me how you came to this dungeon. Neither of us has much time to waste."

Pacing in the cell, Keela recounted the events of the previous day—how she had watched a young boy in a contest of skill and had become attracted to the amulet he wore. When she mentioned the amulet, the hag demanded that Keela describe it fully. Then Keela explained how she had followed the boy to the woodland pool and had stolen his belongings—only to discover she had nothing but a worthless piece of lead to show for her trouble.

"I started to look for the golden amulet," added the thief, "but then I ran into the baroness's thugs. That's how I wound up here. The baroness asked about the amulet and the boy, but I played dumb. End of story. And tomorrow, if I don't get out of here, it'll be the end of me."

Much to Keela's annoyance, the hag began to

cackle with glee.

"I hardly think my story is funny," said the thief.

"Not the tale, my dear, but your failure to see the obvious. Tell me what happened to the boy."

"I don't know," Keela replied, still annoyed. "I never saw him again. As far as I know, he's still in the forest, naked as a jay and angry as a bear. So what do you mean I overlooked the obvious?"

Once again the hag laughed, then fell into a fit of coughing. When it was over, she rasped, "Never in my dreams did I see such good fortune."

"Hey," Keela snapped. "This is more like a nightmare. I'm stuck in a cell with a smelly old blind woman who speaks in riddles, who doesn't know her own name, and who probably doesn't know the way out of here either!" Keela strode to the opposite side of the room, then began to search the wall for passages.

"And you call *me* blind," said the hag. "Exhaustion has clouded your thoughts, Keela. You never lost the amulet. It was in your hands, along with the fate of the boy, and you tossed it to the ground."

"What do you mean?" Keela demanded.

"What you mistook for worthless lead was the very treasure you sought," replied the hag calmly. "And the real treasure is still to be found!"

"Please, stop speaking in circles," said the thief.

"My head is pounding, and I don't understand your nonsense."

"Then I shall tell you a story," said the hag, "and make you understand. . . . Come back and sit beside me."

Too tired to argue, Keela settled down beside the hag.

"Fifteen years ago, I was a midwife," the hag began, "summoned to this castle in the dead of night. I attended Katherine, the duke's wife, who was heavy with child. She was dreadfully ill. In desperation, she whispered to me that the duke's sister, Baroness Von Drek, had poisoned her. The duchess pleaded with me to save her child. As I did so, the duchess passed away.

"When the baroness asked about the fate of the baby, I lied. I told her that the child had never been born. I knew well what the baroness intended—that she would kill this infant boy and promote her own son as heir to the duke's title. So I took the baby into the hills and left him with an old shepherd and his wife. There was nothing to link the baby to this castle but the gift his dying mother had pressed into my hand: a magical amulet . . . seemingly made of lead and glass."

Keela gasped. "*Seemingly*? Are you saying that I robbed the rightful heir to the duchy?"

"It would seem so," the hag replied with a smile.

"But the amulet around his neck was *gold*."

"Yes, because it was around his neck. Because it touched his skin and knew his heart. As I said, the amulet is magical. The duchess had it specially made for her unborn child. In that child's possession, and his possession alone, it reveals its inner beauty. But when it lies elsewhere, the amulet looks like a worthless trinket. The baroness knew about the amulet. When it appeared to be missing, she accused me of stealing it. That's how I became a prisoner in this castle."

"I can't believe it. I robbed the duke's son," sighed Keela. "I always try to stay clear of nobles. That's why I'm in this duchy. Five years ago, I had to escape from King Halvor's guards . . . and now I've done something far worse than raid a royal chicken coop!"

"Don't fret, girl. If you had not robbed the young man, you would not have come to this dungeon—"

"Oh, that's encouraging," Keela interrupted.

"And if you had not come to this dungeon," the hag continued, "you would not be able to restore the duke's son to his rightful position."

"Now, wait a minute," said Keela. "You've got the wrong thief. I just wanted an amulet. Once I'm out of here, I'm not coming back."

"You've forgotten that I am the key to your escape."

"Then I'll find the way out alone."

"That is hardly your destiny, Keela," replied the hag.

"If I follow your advice, I'm destined to be dead," Keela retorted.

"Calm yourself. Didn't you say that you were destined to be tortured in the morning anyway?"

"And that's supposed to make me feel better?"

"Look into your heart, Keela, and do what is right. I will help you escape the castle, but in turn, you must promise to do everything that you can to bring Conor before his father and let the truth be known to all."

"Conor?" asked the thief.

"Conor, the son of Duke Edward," the hag replied. "Keep up with me, child. We haven't got time to waste. Tomorrow night, the baroness is hosting a party here at the castle, celebrating the sixteenth birthday of her son, Rufus. During the party, Duke Edward is expected to name Rufus Von Drek his heir. We cannot let that happen. Now promise me you'll do as I ask!"

"All right, all right," said Keela. "I promise. What choice do I have? Now, please tell me how to get out of here. . . ."

An hour later, Keela found herself perched on a

castle wall, moving along a ledge that was barely as wide as her toes.

"No wonder the hag never escaped," muttered the thief, striving to maintain her balance. Her arms were spread wide, and her fingers lightly gripped the stones. Her face was pressed sideways against the wall, scraping against every ridge in the surface. To make matters worse, a misty rain had begun to fall, making the stonework dangerously slick.

The hag had shown her a secret passage, which wound upward through the wall of the dungeon tower. The passage was just as disgusting as the one she had followed to reach the old woman's cell. It led to a tiny window, barely wide enough for Keela to drop through. She had hung there, half stuck, for several minutes, struggling to descend toward a ledge she was not sure even existed.

Fortunately, it did. Now she was high on the face of the wall that ringed the castle's living quarters, with guards posted overhead on the walkway. Below her lay the moat, and behind that stood the castle's outer fortress. By day, the walls of Durham Castle looked sturdy and proud. Now, stained almost black by the rain, they looked somber and foreboding.

Keela saw a light, streaming from an open window directly ahead of her. It was not a good sign. The ledge Keela was following passed immediately beneath the opening. To avoid being seen, the thief would have to hang from the windowsill, then swing her body back up to the ledge on the other side. In the rain, she doubted it was possible.

She edged toward the window, then leaned in carefully to see whether anyone was inside. Someone was.

A gawky young man was standing before a mirror, admiring himself. His curly orange-red hair formed a bright halo around his freckled face. His bony knees, straining against his tight white leggings, appeared larger than his spindly thighs. Completing the ensemble were a pair of bright red slippers and a short silk shirt, which had enormous purple-and-white puffed sleeves.

The boy picked up a sword, bowed deeply before the mirror, then pointed the blade at the glass. "I, Rufus, do dub thee . . . *Sirrrrr*ufus . . . the Handsome!"

Keela stifled a laugh and eased across the window, hoping "Sir Rufus" would remain absorbed in his own image. The boy dropped the sword and leaned toward the mirror, fixing his gaze on the thief's reflection.

"Hey!" he shouted, turning so quickly that he fell to the floor.

When Rufus reached the window, Keela was

already past the opening, with her face turned away from him. She pressed herself against the wall, hoping the darkness would conceal her.

"Hey!" he shouted again. "Guards! Guards! There's someone on the wall!"

Keela heard men calling out from above. Another man shouted from below. "There! There's the intruder!"

Arrows clattered against the wall beside her head. Keela ducked, then lost her grip, and suddenly she was falling. . . .

Chapter Four

Keela turned herself in the air like a cat. The moat raced up to meet her, and she plunged feetfirst into the brackish water. When the thief resurfaced next to the outer wall, she was gagging. The moat was little better than a sewer into which waste from the castle was dumped. A rat swam past and began to climb her as if she were an island. It squealed as Keela angrily tossed it off. Overhead, she heard the guards shouting. Then she saw the light from a torch. They would find her soon.

"How do I always end up in such a mess?"

muttered the thief.

She swam silently toward the outlet of the moat, holding her head above the water. It did not surprise her to see two guards waiting upon the drawbridge, one with a blazing torch, the other with a crossbow held at the ready. She had no choice. Choking back her disgust, she dived beneath the surface of the swill.

One corner of the moat was barred and screened. Keela searched the bars with her hands until she found an opening in the screen and wriggled through. Her eyes burned fiercely, and her lungs felt as if they would explode. Still, she forced herself to stroke five times before she resurfaced. She had made it into the river from which the water in the moat was drawn. The thief swam to a floating log and clung to it, then let the current carry her down the stream.

When at last she dragged herself, cold and exhausted, onto a bank, the faint light of dawn had begun to glow on the horizon. Keela limped into a clump of bushes, covered herself with leaves, and fell asleep. It had been a rough night.

Two hours later, a warm summer breeze and the gentle hum of insects roused the thief. Keela lay in her hiding place, watching the sunlight dance through the leafy bower overhead. A crow landed in

A scene from the DRAGON STRIKE™ video

a nearby tree and began to chide her.

"You again?" said Keela. "Well, you're absolutely right. What do *I* care who becomes heir to the duchy?"

The crow cawed its reply.

"Hey, no argument here," said the thief. "I've been in that dungeon once. If I do what the hag asks, I'll end up just like her. Or I'll end up dead. Everybody knows you don't mess with nobles—wrong them once and Fate will cut you down twice. Besides, I've been in these parts too long already. Anyone with half a wit can see that I should leave now, just fly away. All right, then. It's the sane thing to do, the smart thing to do, the *only* thing to do. Just get up, Keela, start walking, and don't look back."

But she didn't get up. Instead, she lay there and thought of Conor, who would never know his real father or his birthright. She pictured the baroness, a smug and greedy spider who would soon have the entire duchy in her glistening web.

In the end, though, neither picture persuaded Keela to do as the hag had asked. Another reason weighed more heavily on her mind. Keela had promised to help. And although that promise haunted her now, she could not go back on her word.

The thief rose, brushed herself off, and headed

into the woods. She formed a two-part plan as she walked: find the amulet, then find Conor. The first step seemed easy compared to the second. And what came next—restoring a shepherd to his noble position before the day was over—seemed utterly impossible. Yet there was nothing to do but try.

Keela returned to the great oak where she had tossed the amulet. Finding it proved simple enough. It still lay in the moss between the massive roots, alongside Conor's clothes. She winced at the thought of him spending a cold night in the forest, shrouded in leaves like an animal, even though her own sleep had been much the same. But he was not the thief Keela had presumed him to be, and *she* was the cause of his discomfort.

The clothing provided a clue, however. If Conor had not found his clothes, then perhaps he had looked for some others in the village. Keela still had his coin purse, so he was also penniless. In the village, he might enter another contest to win a prize. At any rate, the village was as good a place as any to start the search for him. Keela pocketed the amulet and tied Conor's other belongings into a bundle, which she slung over her shoulder.

On the way, she decided to make a detour. Despite having two sets of clothes, she felt naked. Her bullwhip was missing. She headed toward where the weasel-faced Darg had clubbed her. If her good luck continued, the whip would lie somewhere at the bottom of the ravine, buried under the leaves. If her luck was bad, of course, then Darg or Titus now had the whip as a souvenir.

After a brief but frantic search, which included a rather unpleasant encounter with a startled snake, Keela found her weapon. She was so thrilled that she kissed the handle and held the whip overhead.

"Thank you, Lady Luck!" shouted the thief. Much to her surprise, someone answered—a man with a deep, booming laugh. It certainly *wasn't* Lady Luck.

"Say, Darg," said the man. "We've found us our little jackrabbit, just where you said we would."

Keela looked up. At the top of the ravine stood Titus, still bandaged across the nose. The weasel-faced Darg was already halfway down the slope, fondling his wooden club. Both men were grinning.

Then Darg sprang toward her. The thief jumped backward and slipped, falling against the opposite bank. Her pursuer laughed. Then he advanced, slapping the club against his free hand while Titus shouted encouragement from above.

Keela glanced at the steep bank behind her. Then she looked at Darg's crazed eyes and his drooling mouth. She couldn't bear the thought of getting clobbered by this creature twice. The thief lashed out at Darg's wrist with her bullwhip and sent the club flying through the air. Then she turned and scrambled up the bank. The chase was on, with both men shouting and cursing behind her.

This time, Keela had the advantage. She had a good lead on Titus, and the whimpering Darg had hesitated, unwilling to follow until he'd picked up his beloved club.

Soon, Keela could hear them no more. She climbed a tree and waited, listening carefully, just to be sure she had lost them. Then she climbed down and slowly made her way toward the village. She knew Darg and Titus might look for her there, but she still had to find Conor.

In the village, the festival continued. The crowds were even greater than the day before. Clearly, the baroness intended her son's sixteenth birthday to be an event everyone in the duchy would long remember.

Onlookers had come from miles around to see what the lady of the castle had arranged. Keela was grateful for their number, since they would make it difficult for the two thugs to find her again. Unfortunately, the crowd would also make it difficult for her to spot Duke Edward's son—assuming he was here at all.

The thief drew the hood of her tunic over her shining copper hair to conceal it from her pursuers. Then she began to wander, looking for any sign of Conor.

Yesterday's crowd had been scant compared to today's, which filled the street with laughter and music. Keela passed a troupe of acrobats and stopped briefly to admire their skill. They had formed a human tower, three men high—which was quite impressive, since each was standing. She wished she had the same bird's-eye view, and thought briefly about seeking one out. But no house or structure in the village rose more than a single story, and standing atop a thatched roof was a sure way to get noticed.

In a nearby field Keela heard men grunting and shouting, and she went to investigate. It was a log-throwing contest. Conor was not among the contenders, though Keela had no doubt he would have fared well.

The fat spectator next to her gnawed on an enormous drumstick. Keela's mouth watered as she watched the juice run down his hand. She had not eaten since the previous morning. The thief wondered briefly if she might snag a piece when he wasn't looking—just a little bite that he might not notice. Then he looked at her and stepped away, like a dog guarding a bone. She forced herself to move on.

In the village green, a theater troupe had erected a stage from the rear of a wagon. Keela stepped into the circle of onlookers, hoping to spy a muscular, blond-haired shepherd among them. An actor with proportions as heroic as Conor's stood upon the stage, stripped to the waist, with a two-handed sword at his side. Three other performers huddled beneath a red tarp, playing the part of a dragon.

The dragon roared and clawed at the hero. The actor clutched his chest with dramatic flair, then fell to his knees. Miraculously, stage blood oozed between his fingers, and the actor smeared it across his breast to enhance the effect.

Then the hero struggled to his feet. "I am Rufus the Bold!" he shouted, raising his sword overhead. "You may tear my flesh and taste my blood, but you shall never quell my courage. In the name of Von Drek, I smite you! For now you shall swallow my steel!"

The actor plunged his sword into the dragon, burying it to the hilt. For what seemed an eternity to Keela, the creature squealed and writhed in agony, as if the red tarp concealed a trio of frantic pigs. Then at last, the beast fell silent. The curtain dropped, and the crowd applauded.

"You mean, 'In the name of *Sirrrrrr*ufus . . . the

Ridiculous,' " muttered the thief as she moved away. The play had obviously been commissioned by the baroness herself.

Once again, Keela began to search the crowd for any sign of the duke's real son. Then, at last, she glimpsed his broad shoulders and his golden hair, moving through the throng far ahead. The crowd closed in, and the image disappeared.

Had she imagined him? Keela's heart began to race. She rushed forward, rudely shoving the others around her aside. The hood fell from her hair, but she made no attempt to replace it. Then the image reappeared: a strapping young man—wearing a flour sack for a tunic and a ridiculously short pair of trousers. He was walking away from her in the distance. Fearing she would lose sight of him again, Keela called out.

"Conor!" she cried. "Conor who comes from the hills!"

The boy turned around. Keela was overjoyed; she had found him at last. Obviously, he did not share her enthusiasm. When he spied the thief, his brows knit together and his mouth dropped to form a scowl. He strode toward Keela like a maniac bent on murder. Then he pulled up short.

"Look out!" Conor yelled.

Keela wheeled—and came face-to-face with the

drooling Darg. She lunged left and saw Titus just a
few yards away. Then she lunged right and spotted
another guard moving toward her through the
crowd. As impossible as it seemed, Darg and Titus
had a friend, and all three men were closing fast.

Chapter Five

Keela wheeled just in time to see Darg's club poised above her head. As she staggered back toward Conor, the club hissed past her ear. Darg grinned and raised his weapon again, preparing to inflict another blow.

Then Keela heard Conor shout a warning: "Duck!"

The thief instantly dropped to her knees. Something whooshed overhead, and she saw a rock hit Darg squarely between the eyes. It landed with a hollow *thwack*, as if it had struck a melon. Darg's

club slipped from his hand. He clutched his fore-
head, too stunned to utter a sound. Then he crossed
his eyes, staggered forward, and fell squarely on top
of Keela. She collapsed beneath his weight.

Somewhere off to her left Keela heard Titus yell
excitedly. "Get the boy, Murdox! The boy!" Then his
voice became low and even. "I'll take care of the
girl. . . ."

The thief struggled to get up, but Darg's body
had pinned her. She could see Titus's legs approaching, and she imagined his sword overhead, ready to
cleave her skull. Then Keela flattened herself and
wriggled free.

Titus was closing in too fast. The thief rose to her
knees and spun around, swinging a leg toward her
attacker. She hooked him squarely behind the
ankles. The big man's feet flew out from underneath
him, and he crashed to the ground beside her. Keela
heard a sharp *smack* as his head struck something
hard. It was Darg's club. Titus's eyes rolled back in
his skull until only the whites showed between his
lids. A dark stain appeared in the dust beneath his
head, then his body went limp.

When the thief looked up, she saw Conor facing
the guard called Murdox. The guard was advancing
through the crowd, shoving startled onlookers
aside. His sword was held high. Conor looked

around in desperation. Keela guessed that he had no weapon.

She grabbed Titus's broadsword and called out Conor's name, then she sent the sword flying through the air. Much to her dismay, Conor's eyes widened like a frightened calf's. As the sword tumbled hilt over blade toward his head, he just stood there, and Keela feared she would be the cause of his death instead of his salvation. Then his arm shot up. Miraculously, he caught the sword by the hilt—just as Murdox came upon him.

The guard slashed at Conor. The boy staggered backward, flailing with his sword. The guard slashed a second time. Again Conor retreated, making a pathetic attempt to defend himself. Apparently he had never held a heavy blade before, or, if he had, he had done so badly. The tip of Murdox's sword found Conor's chest, and Keela saw a faint red streak through the tear in his makeshift tunic. Conor backed into a vendor's tent. He had nowhere to turn, and the thief held her breath.

Conor made a desperate move: he pitched his sword at his attacker. Murdox paused to block the attack. The two swords clanged as steel hit steel, then Conor's sword fell to the ground.

Murdox laughed heartily and kicked the blade aside. In that moment, Conor grabbed the wooden pole holding up a nearby tent. The guard side-stepped quickly and watched the canvas settle harmlessly beside him, covering a screaming vendor.

Conor was still in action. He swung the tent pole like a staff, striking the end against his attacker's skull. It landed with a *crack*. He swiftly reversed his swing of the staff, bringing the other end forward for a second blow. Murdox began to stagger, stunned by the rapid assault on his head.

Keela smiled. Clearly, a staff was this shepherd's weapon of choice. Then she heard Titus moaning behind her. The thief looked for her whip—and saw the handle protruding from beneath Darg's unconscious body. She leaped toward the whip and began to pull.

Before Keela could free her weapon, a big, hairy arm clamped around her neck. The thief was lifted from behind. She reached up to grab her attacker's finger—and felt a blade pressed against her ribs.

"Go ahead and try it," Titus breathed in her ear, pressing the dagger still farther. "Break that finger, and it'll be the last thing you ever do."

Keela tucked her chin against her chest to keep from passing out. She looked down at the knife stuck in her ribs, and hoped it was only a flesh wound.

"Titus, old buddy," she squeaked. "How are ya, handsome?"

A scene from the DRAGON STRIKE™ video

Titus tightened his grip and breathed heavily on her cheek. "Shut up or die," he retorted.

A loud *crack* sounded from the direction of the vendor's tent. Keela saw Murdox sag toward the ground, with Conor's staff against the back of his head. Then the guard lay sprawled on the dirt, unconscious.

Keela's eyes met Conor's. She looked for reassurance, but instead she saw only hatred as the shepherd slowly approached her, swinging his staff like a baton.

Titus growled at Conor. "Don't come any closer, or I'll stick her through the heart," he said, pressing his dagger into Keela's skin.

Conor smiled and took another step forward. "What makes you think I care?" he replied coolly. "She's just a thief to me."

Keela's heart sank. Once again, she was on her own, but it was a position she knew well.

First things first, she thought. Get rid of the knife, then clobber the boy. . . .

The thief looked for a weakness in her captor's hold and found it. She reached out and grabbed the thumb that held the dagger, then twisted it sharply away from her body. Titus's wrist was forced to follow. He cried out in agony. His hand opened, and the dagger fell to the ground.

Titus threw Keela to the dirt like a rag doll. Then the thief heard Conor's war cry and saw him charge toward Titus, pointing the tent pole at his enemy.

Conor swung his staff, but Titus raised an arm to block the attack. Titus began a punch with his free hand, but it was too late—Conor had already reversed the staff's swing, bringing the opposite end into Titus's stomach. The guard doubled over in pain. Conor finished him with a blow to the back of the head, and Titus collapsed for the second time.

Keela sat in the dirt, too stunned to rise. She looked at her aching side. It bled, but the wound wasn't serious. Then Conor was beside her.

"Are you all right?" he asked.

She nodded.

"Then get up," he said gruffly, grabbing her forearm. "They won't stay unconscious forever. And who knows who'll show up next."

"Wait!" Keela yelled as he dragged her to her feet. "My bullwhip!"

She scrambled toward Darg's body. The man moaned as she pulled the weapon free. Conor spotted the bundle of clothing Keela had dropped—his own clothing—and snatched it up. Then he grabbed Keela's hand and led her into the forest.

They traveled for several minutes before Conor stopped. Keela started to talk, but he held a finger to his lips and listened for the sound of pursuit.

Keela clutched her wounded side and tried to catch her breath. "I'm sure no one followed," she said hoarsely, "not one of those three, anyway. Thanks for helping me."

To her surprise, Conor turned and pushed her to the ground. Then he sat on her stomach and pinned her arms. She cried out in pain.

"Get this straight," he growled. "I helped you for one reason only—to be rid of those thugs myself. Now where's my amulet?"

"In my pocket!" cried Keela. "You don't have to fight me for it. I was bringing it to you."

"A likely story," Conor replied. "Hand it over." He let go of Keela's arms and moved aside.

Keela fumbled for the amulet in her tunic and presented it to Conor. He slipped it over his head, and at once it turned to gold.

"I'd say thank you," grumbled the boy, "except it was mine in the first place." He rose to his feet and turned away.

"Where are you going?" Keela yelled.

"Home," he replied. "My parents warned me that the lowlands were filled with liars and thieves. And—may they rest in peace—they were right."

Keela rose and staggered after him. "Oh, no, you don't. I've climbed through tunnels, fallen in a moat, romped with rats, swam a river, and took the end of a knife just to help you. You can't walk away now."

"*Help* me?" said Conor. "You mean help yourself to my belongings." He glanced over his shoulder. "And don't be so dramatic. You've only got a flesh wound."

"I don't care what any old shepherd and his wife told you," said Keela.

The boy stopped in his tracks.

Keela continued to rant. "You still don't know a thing—nothing important, anyway, like how to recognize a true friend. Or who your *real* parents were!"

The boy turned around. He looked stunned. "What are you saying?" he asked.

"I'm saying the people who raised you weren't really your parents."

"*I* know that," Conor said quickly. "Eric and Josephine were old enough to be my grandparents. The question is, how did *you* know that?"

"Because I've met your mother's murderer," said Keela.

"That's a lie," Conor replied angrily, "just another one of your lies. My real mother was a foreigner. She was weak from travel, and she died in childbirth while crossing the mountains. Eric and Josephine said they tried to save her."

"Why would I lie about something this important?" asked the thief. "Your mother did die in childbirth, but not in the mountains, Conor. She died in a castle, where she was poisoned by Baroness Von Drek. Your mother was Duke Edward's wife—and you are his only son!"

Conor stared at her in disbelief. "That's ridiculous. Eric and Josephine wouldn't have lied to me."

"Maybe they didn't know who you were, Conor. Or maybe they died before they got a chance to tell you the truth—I don't know. But they had proof of who you are—and that proof is around your neck."

"Well, at least you've got one thing right," said Conor slowly. "Eric and Josephine did say this amulet was from my mother, and that I should guard it closely. . . ."

"See!" Keela cried.

"But that doesn't prove your story. It doesn't prove anything at all."

"By the heavens!" cried Keela. "You are the most stubborn, pigheaded person I've ever met. That amulet is special. Only a noble could afford such a thing. I have nothing to gain by telling you the truth. But you have everything to lose by not believing it!"

"I don't care about being rich," said Conor. "You can't trick me with greed—that works only on the likes of you."

"I'm not talking about gold and silver, you dolt," Keela snapped. "If you turn your back on your birthright, you'll never know your real father. The idiot son of the baroness will take your place as Duke Edward's heir—and his mother will have complete power over him. This duchy will be overrun with thugs . . . thugs just like the ones in the village. Hundreds of people will suffer. And it will all be your fault!"

Conor stared at Keela, then walked over and grabbed her shoulders. He pulled her close and looked her straight in the eyes, as if searching for an answer.

Keela struggled for something else to say, anything else to convince him, but the words caught in her throat. Her heart pounded, and her legs suddenly felt weak.

Then Conor loosened his grip. "You'd better not be lying," he said.

"I swear to you, I'm not," Keela said softly. "And if you'll come with me, I can prove it."

Chapter Six

W here are we going?" Conor asked as Keela led the way through the woods. "To Duke Edward's castle," Keela replied. "There's someone you should meet."

Conor frowned. "Oh, sure," he said, "I'll just walk up to Duke Edward and say, 'Well met, sir. I'm your son Conor. And this is Keela. Keep an eye on your jewelry.'"

"Don't be silly," Keela replied. "I didn't mean Duke Edward. He thinks his son was never born. Besides, he wouldn't grant us an audience—

Baroness Von Drek would see to that."

"Then who?" asked Conor.

"A very wise old woman. She's the only person who knows what happened the night you came into this world—besides the baroness, of course."

"And this old woman lives in the castle?" Conor asked.

"Sort of," said the thief. "She's been a prisoner in the dungeon for about fifteen years. That dungeon is a horrid place, Conor—believe me, I know. She hasn't fared well. So I figure we'll just have to help her escape."

Conor laughed. "You must be crazy," he said. "Haven't you ever heard of the castle guard?"

"Of course," Keela replied. "In fact, we're fairly well acquainted. But that old hag is the midwife who saved you, Conor. I'm sure she can prove who you are. Besides, I've got a plan. And with both of us working together, what could go wrong?"

Conor looked at Keela and shook his head. "Now I'm sure you're crazy. But I guess I am, too, since I'm beginning to believe your story. So what's your plan?"

"First, we take care of your clothes," she said, pointing to his flour-sack tunic and his ill-fitting pants. "I've seen poorly dressed peasants before, but you look ridiculous."

Conor frowned as he swung the bundle containing his belongings from his shoulder. "Are you forgetting how I ended up this way?"

Keela winked. "Hardly," she said.

Conor's face reddened, and he ducked behind a tree to change. "Don't peek," he admonished.

"Boy," teased Keela from the other side, "you sure are shy?"

"And you're pretty brazen for a girl," Conor replied, stepping out in his old attire. "It's hardly ladylike. And it's pretty annoying, too. I'll have you know it was no fun rounding up that flour sack—or stealing those pants from a scarecrow."

"Why, sir," Keela said sweetly. "That's twice you've called me pretty. But enough small talk. Come on. We've got to sneak into the castle."

"How?" asked Conor, following her through the woods.

"I'm still working on a few details," replied the thief.

Keela paused. The pair had reached a dirt road at the edge of the forest. They crouched behind a mass of shrubs and peered through the branches.

In the distance loomed Durham Castle, the duke's home. It looked much cheerier than it had the night before. Stout gray towers guarded each corner of its outer wall. Within, the graceful towers of the central keep soared higher still. Every tower was topped by bright purple-and-white pennants, wafting in the breeze. On the far side of the castle lay the river in which Keela had swum. It sparkled as it snaked toward the horizon. The thief couldn't see the moat, but she remembered it well.

A wagon passed on the road, carrying a load of squawking chickens. Soon came another, bearing a half dozen barrels of ale.

"Those must be supplies for the baroness's special party," Conor said. "I heard about it in the village. She invited more than a hundred nobles and wealthy merchants from miles around just to celebrate her son's birthday tonight. It's the big finish to this week's celebration."

"Now I know how we'll get into the castle," said Keela, smiling slyly.

She pointed to an approaching wagon, drawn by a pair of gray nags. Seated at the front of the wagon was a plump, jolly-faced man. Two large wooden crates were stacked beside him on the wagon seat, one precariously atop the other. Each crate held a white goose. The man was singing a ballad about a "sassy lassie" called Nellie, and he was badly off key. Every now and then a goose would honk in complaint. A mountain of dried herbs and straw was piled in the back of the wagon, half covered by a tarp.

"That load is definitely headed to the castle," said Keela. "The herbs will probably be used to freshen the Great Hall. Feel like catching a ride?"

"Good idea," Conor replied.

As the wagon passed, they slipped out of the woods. Keela leaped into the rear of the wagon without making a sound. She ducked low, so the driver couldn't see her over the mound of hay. Conor clambered in beside her with a thud, but the driver didn't seem to notice. He continued to sing off key: "Oh, Nellie, Nellie, you've such a fine belly, and teeth so white and strong . . ."

Keela wondered whether it was a love song or an ode to a horse. She leaned close to Conor. "Try to hide near the driver," she whispered. "If a guard searches the load, he'll probably just poke at the back once or twice. When we get safely inside the wall, we'll jump out."

Conor nodded. The thief made her way toward the front of the wagon, crawling low along the side. When she looked back, the boy was already hidden. Keela burrowed under the herbs and hay like a field mouse. Her nose tickled, but she stifled the urge to sneeze.

When they reached the drawbridge, the wagon drew to a halt. Keela hid just behind the wagon seat, under the tarp. She heard the driver greet a guard.

A scene from the DRAGON STRIKE™ video

"How are you, Joseph?" asked the driver cheerfully. "What do you think of my gift?"

"Looks like two fine geese," replied the guard.

"Beg your pardon?" asked the driver.

"I said, *looks like two fine geese*," bellowed the guard.

"My finest," answered the man. "They'll be on the duke's table tonight for sure."

The geese began to honk more loudly, as if they suddenly understood their fate. The horses snorted and stomped, rocking the wagon.

"Whoa," said the driver soothingly. "Easy, girls . . . those ganders will do you no harm."

The guard gave his okay for the wagon to proceed across the drawbridge. Keela breathed a sigh of relief. In a few moments, the wagon would reach the castle's outer court, which was almost as big as the village square, and usually just as crowded. It should be easy to slip away from the wagon unnoticed once the driver came to a stop.

Then the hopeful picture in Keela's mind disappeared. Conor sneezed.

"Halt!" cried the guard.

"What is it, Joseph?" asked the driver.

"Didn't you hear that?"

"Hear what?" said the man on the wagon.

"I'm not sure," replied the guard. "I'd better check

your load." He called for another guard to assist.

Keela heard something poking through the straw behind her. When she turned, she glimpsed a sword withdrawing. She edged toward the driver, until she was directly under his seat and could see the back of his legs. The thief knew Conor could be discovered at any moment. She had to act fast.

Keela noticed the wooden crate overhead. It was too large to fit squarely on the wagon seat, and about a quarter of the crate's bottom overhung the front. The thief remembered that a second crate was stacked on top. She withdrew a pick from her tunic and held her breath. Then she stuck the driver hard in the calf. As he yowled and sprang to his feet, she shoved the crate with her other hand.

Both crates crashed to the ground, releasing a pair of hissing, flapping ganders. The gray nags bolted forward, racing across the drawbridge and through the open gate. Keela heard the driver scream as he lost his balance and fell from the wagon. She peered out from her hiding place—and saw the wagon heading straight for a wall!

"Jump!" she yelled.

The thief leaped out as the wagon careened violently and tipped, spilling its contents onto a group of stable hands. Suddenly, Conor was beside her on the ground. Together they rushed through the startled onlookers and slipped through an open door.

They found themselves in the chapel of Durham Castle. For the moment, at least, it was empty.

"Do you think anyone followed us?" Keela whispered as they crouched behind a pew.

"Maybe not," said Conor quietly. "Everyone was scattering."

"Then let's move before someone does."

She went to a door in the corner. It was locked, but that wasn't a problem for a thief. Keela picked the lock in less than a minute. Conor was right behind her as they slipped into a dark, narrow corridor that led to a circular stairway made of stone.

"Which way?" Conor whispered.

"Down," said Keela. "I think I know how to reach the dungeon from here."

Slowly, carefully, they made their way down the stairs. When they reached the bottom, they heard voices. Keela peeked around the corner. Two guards stood in the hall before an iron-barred door. They were orcs—rather stupid creatures who resembled hunchbacked men with pointy pink ears, reddish eyes, and gray-green skin. Their noses looked like wet, glistening pig snouts.

Keela waved Conor back with her hand. They climbed a few steps until they were safely out of earshot.

"There are two of them," whispered Keela, "but Lady Luck is on our side today. They're orcs. Looks like they're armed with clubs." She pulled her bullwhip from her belt. "I'll try to draw them past the bottom of the stairs," she said.

Conor smiled and nodded.

Holding her bullwhip behind her back, the thief stepped silently into the hall at the base of the steps, then tiptoed backward. The hall was dark. Keela pressed herself into the shadows.

"Pssst!"

One of the orcs snorted. "Didya hear that, Grug?" he asked.

Keela stepped into the faint light and motioned with her index finger. "Psst! Over here, fellas," she said.

"Hey!" shouted the orc. "There's a girl over there! Let's get her!" Both orcs raced down the corridor.

Keela turned and ran. As the first orc passed the stairwell, Conor's foot flew out. The orc tripped and crashed to the ground, and his companion stumbled on top of him. As the pair thrashed about in confusion, Conor stepped out and seized a club, then knocked each guard on the head as if he were cracking two coconuts. The fight was over before it had begun.

Both guards lay sprawled on the floor, out cold.

Keela stood in the corridor, smiling. "Nice work," she said, tucking her whip back into her belt. "I barely had to lift a finger." She began to search the orcs.

"Hey!" Conor whispered. "Speaking of lifting—this is no time for petty theft!"

Keela frowned. "I'm not stealing anything, you dolt," she retorted. "I was borrowing *these*." She dangled a set of keys before the boy's nose. "Or didn't you think they would come in handy?"

Conor smiled. "I didn't think a girl with *your* talents actually needed keys," he said teasingly.

Keela ignored the comment. She used the keys to open the door at the end of the corridor. Together, she and Conor began searching for the old midwife.

The first cell was empty, so Conor went back into the hall. In a moment, he returned, dragging both orcs. When the guards were snoring safely inside, Keela locked the cell.

The next room held a madman, who leaped to the door and pressed his face to the bars as they passed, snarling and frothing like a rabid dog.

Finally, Keela and Conor found the cell they were seeking. The thief opened the door, and the pair went inside.

"Who's there?" asked the hag.

"It's Keela," replied the thief. "I've brought someone with me."

The hag chuckled. "Come here, boy," she said. "Let me feel your face." She sounded as if she were greeting an old friend.

Conor was startled by her familiar tone, but he did as the woman asked. "Keela has told me about you," he said. "She says you can prove I'm the son of the duke."

"Of course you are," said the hag. She explored his face with her hands. "As surely as you are the son of the duke's beloved wife. You seem very much like your mother, Conor. She was not much older than you when she died. Have you got the amulet?"

Conor took it from around his neck and handed it to the old woman. At once, the golden strands turned to dull gray lead, and the blue stone became a disk made of glass.

"It's been a very long time since I held this," the hag whispered, exploring the face of the amulet with her fingers. "But your mother told me its secret. Watch carefully." She traced her dirt-stained hand along the metal swirls, making three tiny circles.

Keela heard a faint click, and the front of the amulet fell open. Behind the glass stone lay an inscription. The hag handed the amulet to Conor.

"What does it say?" Keela asked.

Conor answered in a hoarse whisper. "It says, 'For my firstborn son.' And beneath that it's signed 'Lady Katherine.'"

"What did I tell you?" said Keela excitedly. "Katherine was the duke's wife!"

"I thought that was obvious," rasped the hag. "And this is no time for idle chatter. In less than an hour, Duke Edward will name his sister's son his heir. We must find a way to stop him!"

Chapter Seven

R ight," said Keela. "Let's get started."

Conor helped the hag to her feet. "It's time you got out of this cell," he said.

"I agree," added the thief. "I couldn't stand one night in this rat-infested dungeon—and she's been here for years!"

The old woman thanked them. Slowly, they made their way out into the hall and up the circular stairs. When they reached the top, the hag was weak and gasping for breath. Conor picked up her small form and carried her into the chapel as if she were a child. He placed her gently upon a pew.

71

"Where are we?" rasped the old woman.

"In the castle's house of worship," Keela replied.

"Then you must leave me now," whispered the woman.

Keela started to protest, but the woman raised a quaking hand and touched it to Keela's lips.

"Do not argue," said the hag. "I will be all right here. Your task is difficult enough without an old woman to slow you down. You and Conor must find a way to see Duke Edward. Show him the amulet. Tell him the story of Conor's birth, as I have told it to you."

"We'll come back for you," said Keela.

"Yes, I know you will," said the old woman, lying down upon the pew. "And I will be waiting. Remember your promise, Keela. You must do everything you can to help Conor regain his birthright. But beware of the baroness. She has murdered before, and she will not hesitate to kill again to get what she wants."

Keela shuddered, remembering the baroness's long red nails and her wicked smile. More than anything, the thief wanted to see that smile wiped away.

"Soon," said the thief, "you won't have to worry about *anyone* named Von Drek."

The hag patted Keela on the hand. "Do not be too harsh with the baroness's son," she whispered. "He cannot help who his mother is, and he may not share her evil desires."

"I've seen him in action," said Keela. "He's definitely not as smart. But that's how the baroness keeps him under her thumb."

Conor touched the thief gently on the arm.

"We have to hurry," he said.

Keela nodded and quickly followed him into the courtyard.

"I'm afraid that old woman won't live much longer," said the thief.

"Maybe not," said Conor, "but, thanks to you, at least she won't die in a dungeon."

Outside, the court was full of people, wagons, and horses. Workers hurried past. Bosses shouted commands. Soldiers stood at their posts on the wall, watching over the scene. In fact, it seemed that a sentry guarded every door to the keep, the part of the castle in which the duke and baroness resided.

"Now we know why the dungeon was watched so poorly," said Conor. "Every other guard must be here."

"Or in the Great Hall, where the party will take place," said Keela gloomily. "Maybe we can sneak in among the kitchen workers or slip in with some guests. I'll see about the kitchen. You check the main entrance. Then we'll meet back here and make a plan."

Conor nodded. Keela watched him head slowly toward a crowd that had gathered at the main door.

Half the people there were guests. The women wore silk gowns with wide, sweeping skirts. The men were decked in fine cloaks or tunics and expensive leather boots. Some even wore shining armor. Although Conor's own clothes were better than a flour sack, he still looked out of place.

Keela saw a baker carrying a tray of bread from an outdoor oven. She followed him toward a door to the castle—but pulled up short. Titus and Darg were there. Titus no longer had a bandage over his nose, but it was still purple and swollen. Keela rubbed her side, remembering how Titus had pressed the tip of his knife against her ribs. "I should have bitten you much harder," she whispered, "but maybe I'll have another chance."

As Keela watched, Titus stopped a pastry chef whose cart was laden with cakes. Keela heard Titus bellow at the chef, claiming that the cakes had to be inspected. Darg was already stuffing a little cream-filled tart in his mouth. The white filling oozed between his lips and dribbled down his pointy chin.

The chef started to argue with Titus. In response, the towering brute growled and put a hand on his broadsword, and the chef quickly handed him three cakes. Titus stuffed his mouth full, then waved the man past.

The thief headed back to the meeting place, where Conor already waited.

"It doesn't look good," he said. "We can't get in the main door dressed like this. We'll need a disguise to pass as guests."

"So I noticed," Keela said.

"But that's not all," added Conor. "We'll also need an invitation. Everyone admitted to the Great Hall has a scroll bearing the baroness's personal seal. We can't get in without one."

"The kitchen door looks even worse," replied the thief. "Darg and Titus are there, and at least a half dozen other guards are within striking range. Maybe we can find another entrance, or perhaps even a secret passage."

"That would take a long time," said Conor, "and time is not on our side."

Keela turned away in frustration, then noticed a wagon pulling through the castle gate. It was covered and closed, like a gypsy wagon. Bright scenes were painted on the sides. The thief recognized the wagon from the village. It belonged to a theater troupe—the one Keela had seen performing an awful play about "Sir Rufus" and a red dragon.

"I have an idea," she said.

A scene from the DRAGON STRIKE™ video

"I hope it doesn't involve stealing someone's clothes," Conor answered. "I'd hate to rob one of the guests."

"Well, they're not *exactly* guests," Keela replied, "but they do have a lot of clothes." She nodded toward the gaily painted wagon. "How are you at acting?" she asked.

"What do you mean?"

"I'll bet the baroness hired those actors to perform at the party. We'll just take their place. But instead of telling the story the baroness wants to hear, we'll do a different little drama—about a duchess who is poisoned and a baby who is saved."

"I don't know . . ." said Conor.

Keela stepped closer to Conor, taking his arm. "Trust me," she said. "This plan is so great, someday the best bard in the kingdom will write about it. Besides, have you got a better idea?"

Sadly, Conor had to admit that he did not.

"Great," said Keela. "Then let's get started. The show must go on. And soon it'll be curtains for the Baroness Von Drek!"

Chapter Eight

The thief studied the approaching wagon. The handsome actor who had played Rufus in the village held the reins. Beside him sat a very pretty brunette, roughly Keela's age. She smiled at the actor adoringly. He whispered something in her ear, and she began to giggle.

Keela turned toward Conor. "I saw four performers in the village," she said. "That fellow who's driving, for one, and then three others. That means two actors must be in the wagon."

"Four's a pretty big number," said Conor, "even if

one of them is female."

"Not if we tackle them two at a time," Keela said.

To her annoyance, she saw Conor staring at the dark-haired actress. "*I'll* take care of the girl when the time comes," she added.

Conor smiled and raised an eyebrow. "Jealous?" he teased.

Keela felt herself blush, and that annoyed her even more. "Don't flatter yourself," she retorted. "Just follow my lead."

As the wagon passed, the thief sprang onto the back, holding a slender silver pick in her hand. It turned out she didn't need it—the door wasn't locked. She swung it open and jumped inside.

The thief did a double take. The back of the wagon was filled to the ceiling with trunks and costumes. Seated atop one trunk were two startled and scrawny little men with pale, wispy hair—each identical to the other. They stared at Keela with wide eyes and open mouths, like a pair of newborn birds. The thief tried hard not laugh.

"Who—who are you?" asked one man, quaking.

"I work for the baroness," said Keela matter-of-factly.

Conor stepped in behind her, gently closing the door.

"And this is my personal assistant," Keela added.

"The baroness has ordered us to inspect your wagon."

The second man stammered out a protest. "B-B-But, we haven't even stopped moving. . . ."

"The baroness doesn't like to waste time," said Keela harshly, "and neither do we. Now, do as I say and you won't get hurt."

"Oh, Siril!" whispered the first man. "They're robbers!" His hands shot straight up into the air. The second man surrendered, too, like a reflection in a mirror.

The thief shook her head in amazement. She couldn't believe her good luck—she could have handled these fools single-handedly.

"Okay," said the thief, using her most menacing tone possible. "You're right. We *are* robbers. Now keep quiet or—or my friend here will gut you like piglets. Understand?"

Both men nodded quickly.

Conor stepped close to Keela and whispered in her ear. "Piglets?" he said, with a faint smirk on his lips.

"Just play along," Keela whispered. "This'll be easier than I thought."

The thief turned to the frightened men. "First I need some rope, then I need two scarves. Don't get up—just tell me where they are. And remember, keep quiet."

The first man pointed to a trunk without making a sound. Conor opened it and found the items Keela had requested, then handed them to the thief. She tied a scarf over each actor's mouth. Then she commanded them to sit in a corner at the back of the wagon, where she bound their hands and feet.

Suddenly the wagon came to a halt. As if he had read Keela's thoughts, Conor searched about for a weapon. The first trunk he opened held only clothes. In the second one he discovered a wooden mallet—not the best defense, perhaps, but time did not allow a further search. He positioned himself beside the door.

The thief turned to the first little man. She smiled sweetly and said, "I don't want to hurt you, but I will if you don't do exactly as I say. Do you understand?"

The man nodded.

Keela removed his gag. "What's your name?" she asked.

"Elbert," squeaked the man. "And that's my brother, Siril. We're twins."

"I never would have guessed," said the thief dryly. "Now, Elbert, I want you to call your friends." She placed her hand on his throat. "And *no* tricks."

The little man opened his mouth, but he was too frightened to speak. No sound came out.

Then someone pounded on the wall. "We're here,

lads!" boomed a hearty voice. "Come on up front!"

Keela put a finger to Elbert's lips. "Tell him you need help, and that he and the girl should come back here."

This time, Elbert managed to speak. "Uh . . . Roderick? Guendolyn?"

"What is it?" boomed the young man up front.

"We have a teensy-weensy problem," Elbert squeaked. "Could you help?"

Roderick groaned in dismay. "*What* problem?" he asked.

Elbert looked at Keela searchingly. "What should I say?" he whispered. "That some guests dropped by?"

Keela rolled her eyes. "Not if you want to live," she replied tersely. "Just say you have to *show* him the problem. And be convincing."

Elbert shook with fear. "R-R-Roderick?" he stammered. "You r-r-really and truly should see this. Honest."

Roderick groaned again. "All right, all right . . . You guys are nothing but trouble!"

The thief stuffed the gag back into Elbert's mouth, then stood and pressed her back against the rear wall of the wagon, opposite Conor.

The back door opened. The burly actor who had been driving stepped through the door.

"What's the problem *this* time?" he demanded.

Before Roderick could react, Conor pulled him into the wagon and struck him on the back of the head with the mallet. The actor sprawled on the floor, rocking the wagon.

"Sorry, fellow," said Conor. "You'll be out for a while."

Then Guendolyn stepped into the doorway. When she saw the actor on the floor, her mouth dropped open. Before Guendolyn could scream, Keela leaped from her hiding place and clasped a hand over the girl's mouth. They struggled. The thief fell backward, wrestling the actress to the wagon's floor. Conor sidestepped and shut the door.

The actress thrashed wildly. She kicked Keela hard in the shin and tried to bite her hand. The thief brought her arm around the girl's neck and began to squeeze.

"Quit struggling, you idiot," Keela snapped. "I'm just trying to make you pass out. It's not like I'm trying to kill you!"

Guendolyn took little comfort from Keela's assurance. She continued to thrash, but Keela kept her arm clamped on the girl's throat. Finally, the actress fell unconscious. The thief pushed the limp girl aside and stood up, rubbing her shin.

"You could've helped," she said angrily to Conor.

"I didn't think you needed any," he teased. "After all, you said *you'd* take care of the girl."

"This is no time for jokes," replied Keela. "Let's get to work and find some costumes." She began to search the trunks. After a moment, she drew out a jet-black gown and a dark wig, then she found a small black mask with feathers protruding from the top, like horns. "This looks like a Von Drek costume to me," she said.

"What should I wear?" asked Conor.

"We're going to perform a play about your life," said Keela, "so eventually you'll just be you. That amulet is your best prop of all. But first, take this." She handed him a pillow and a robe. "Put the pillow on your stomach. You'll have to play your own mother."

Conor scoffed. "You want me to play a woman?"

"Who else is going to do it?" Keela asked. "I'm supposed to kill you, remember? Besides, lots of male actors play women." Keela looked at the captives huddled in the corner, shaking like two shorn sheep in a snowdrift. "I'll bet Siril and Elbert have played women," she said. "Am I right, lads?"

Siril and Elbert bobbed their heads in agreement.

"See?" said Keela to Conor. "Now quit your complaining."

The thief began to change into her costume, then

paused. Conor was staring at her, grinning. Keela blushed. "Turn around," she said.

Conor laughed. "Now you know how it feels," he replied. "You're not as fearless as you pretend to be."

Remembering her other audience, Keela draped a scarf over Siril and Elbert's eyes, then changed into the gown. It was a far cry from her usual boyish attire. The dress fit snugly to the waist, then flared broadly.

Conor turned around and let out a low whistle. "You don't look like a villainess," he said.

"I'm not finished," she answered, embarrassed by the attention. She donned the wig and mask. A bit of white powder and red lip-stain from a makeup kit completed her attire—almost. The thief picked up her whip and tucked it under her skirt. "Just in case," she said to Conor. "And I recommend you keep that hammer. Too bad there's no staff in sight."

"I thought your plan was foolproof," Conor replied.

"It is," said Keela, "but it never hurts for us to be prepared."

She stepped over to Elbert and pulled the gag from his mouth. "How were you supposed to get into the Great Hall?" Keela asked.

"Our invitation is in that trunk," answered Elbert meekly.

"Thanks," said Keela, replacing the gag. "You've been a big help."

Conor stepped beside her. "Don't you think we should tie up the other two?" he asked. "And maybe stash them in a trunk for safekeeping?" No sooner had he posed the questions when someone pounded on the back door of the wagon.

"Hey, you in there!" shouted a man. "Come out *now*! Baroness Von Drek wants to see you."

Chapter Nine

The thief opened the door just far enough to poke her head out. A guard was standing outside. He looked very unhappy.

Keela smiled agreeably. "Did you knock?" she asked.

"Yer late," snarled the man. "The baroness says you should've started your play ten minutes ago."

"Sorry, sir," the thief replied. "We, uh, had a few loose ends to tie up, but we're ready now."

"Let me see your papers," demanded the guard.

Keela showed him the scroll that Elbert had provided.

The guard looked at it briefly, then handed it back to her. "Follow me," he said.

Keela and Conor slipped out of the wagon and pulled the door shut behind them.

"I thought there were four of you," said the guard.

"Siril and Elbert are sick," Keela replied quickly.

The guard grumbled. "The baroness won't be happy, but there's nothing to do about it now. You've already been announced." He led them into the keep. Conor pulled the hood of his robe over his head, partly concealing his face.

When they reached the Great Hall, Keela looked at the room in awe. The vaulted ceiling rose two stories. Tapestries hung from the walls, depicting scenes of hunting and conquest. Herbs covered the stone floor. More than a hundred guests sat at the heavy wooden tables lining the sides of the room. Peasant girls flitted about the chamber, pouring ale and bringing food, like bees at work in a flower bed.

In the center of the Great Hall stood a small stage. Directly before it lay another table. Keela shuddered. Baroness Von Drek was seated in the middle, sipping red wine from a silver chalice. On her left sat Rufus, grinning stupidly. On her right sat Duke Edward. He was a handsome, gray-haired man, but he looked rather sad and bored.

A scene from the DRAGON STRIKE™ video

When the baroness noticed the two actors, she waved her hand at the guard escorting them. "Wait here," he grumbled. The guard stepped over to the baroness. She whispered something in his ear, then the guard returned.

"Baroness Von Drek would like to have a word with you, miss," he said to Keela.

The thief's heart began to pound like a drum. Had the baroness recognized her despite the costume? Forcing herself to remain calm, she approached the center table and curtseyed.

Baroness Von Drek leaned across the table and whispered hoarsely. "This does not look like the play I commissioned for Rufus," she hissed. "Where are the other actors? And why is that one wearing a robe? He should be in a full suit of armor!"

"That will come later, Lady Von Drek," answered Keela, trying to disguise her voice. Then she spoke louder, so that Rufus was sure to overhear. "First, in honor of your son's birthday, we have prepared a special surprise!"

"I love surprises!" cried Rufus.

"Well, I do not," snapped the baroness.

But Rufus had already sprung to his feet, holding his glass high. "Everyone!" he cried. "It's time for my birthday drama!" The crowd quieted, though not completely.

The thief returned to the stage and took her place next to Conor. "I'll narrate," she said softly. "You just play along."

Conor nodded, but he did not look at Keela. Instead, he stared at Duke Edward and the baroness.

"Begin the drama!" shouted a man to the left, sloshing ale from his mug.

Keela stepped forward. Her stomach was churning, and her throat was parched. She coughed, then began to speak. "Uh . . . it was a dark and stormy night. . . ."

"Speak up! I can't hear you!" shouted Rufus.

Keela started again, raising her voice. "Once upon a time, there lived a woman who was heavy with child. She was much beloved."

Keela gestured toward Conor. He bowed deeply. When he stood up, his hood fell away, revealing his boyish locks. Conor struggled to replace the hood, then the pillow fell from beneath his robe. The audience roared.

"Ooh!" exclaimed Rufus. "A farce!"

The thief's heart fell. If the people thought the drama was a comedy, they might not take her words seriously. She began anew: "Outside, lightning crashed and thunder boomed, for the heavens knew that something evil was afoot in—"

"Stop the play!" A man was shouting in the back

of the room. "Stop the play! They're impostors!"

The thief looked toward the sound. Roderick was at the door, rubbing his head. Beside him stood Siril and Elbert, still wide-eyed, and Guendolyn, who was livid.

Baroness Von Drek sprang to her feet. She stared at Keela intently. Then a look of horror washed over her face. "You!" she cried. She pointed her bony white finger toward Keela and Conor. "Guards! Seize them both!"

Men in armor began to swarm toward the stage. Conor landed a blow with his hammer, but before he could swing again, two men grabbed him from behind, pinning his arms. A third guard stood before him, pressing the tip of his sword to Conor's throat. "Don't move, boy," warned the guard, "or you'll lose more than your vocal cords."

Keela withdrew her bullwhip and leaped onto the table in front of the baroness. She began to aim for the sword at Conor's throat—but then she had a better idea. The thief lashed at Conor's shirt. The whip tore the fabric open, revealing the golden amulet on his chest.

"Look, Duke Edward!" shouted Keela. "This is your son, and the amulet can pro—"

"What nonsense is this?" snapped the baroness. She shoved Keela from behind and sent the thief sprawling onto the floor.

Keela struggled to speak, but the wind was knocked from her lungs.

"Guards!" shouted Baroness Von Drek. "Must I do everything myself? Seize this girl—and if she dares to interrupt my son's party again, cut her throat!"

The thief tried to rise, but a guard held her down firmly.

Baroness Von Drek walked over to Conor and spat in his face. She seized the amulet from around his neck. Instantly, it turned to lead in her hand.

"Now take these thieves from my sight!" hissed the baroness. "To the dungeon!"

A man's voice boomed behind her.

"Wait! Bring them to me." Duke Edward rose from the table. "And take those blades away from their throats. We are still civil in this castle."

A guard helped Keela to her feet, then led her before the duke. Conor was placed beside her.

"Edward!" shrieked the baroness. "They are criminals. Do not let them spoil poor Rufus's birthday."

"Be quiet, Ursula," replied the duke. "Bring me the amulet."

"This cheap bauble?" squawked the baroness. Reluctantly, she placed it in his hand. "Why, it is only a bit of costume jewelry!"

"Indeed . . ." said the duke dryly. "Then why did it interest you so?" He did not wait for her reply. Instead, he walked over to Conor and showed him the amulet.

"Where did you get this?" he asked.

"From my mother," Conor replied, "but she died the night I was born."

The duke stared into Conor's eyes. "Your mother," he said softly.

"Show him the inscription, Conor," said the thief hoarsely, struggling to regain her voice. "Open the amulet."

The duke nodded to the guards holding Conor's arms. They released the boy. When Conor took the amulet, it turned to shining gold. The guests at the head table gasped. Conor traced his fingers over the amulet three times, just as the hag had done. The amulet fell open, revealing the message: *For my first-born son.* It was signed *Lady Katherine.*

"It's a trick!" cried the baroness. "They are nothing but charlatans. Do not let yourself be duped, dear brother!"

"I asked you to be quiet, Ursula," boomed the duke. "Now do as I command."

The baroness fell silent.

Duke Edward stepped over to Keela. "What is

your story, girl?" he asked.

"I'm not an actress," said Keela quickly.

The duke smiled. "That is obvious," he replied. "What prompted you to pretend you are?"

"I wanted you to meet Conor, your rightful heir—and to know that your own sister poisoned your wife!"

"Liar!" cried the baroness. But when she saw the look of contempt in her brother's eyes, her mouth snapped shut. Her thin, stretched lips twisted into a crooked and guilty smile. She took a step backward, then another. Suddenly she snatched up her voluminous black skirt and dashed toward the door. Duke Edward waved at a guard, who easily intercepted the woman. The baroness stared at the duke in shock and disbelief, but she made no further attempt to flee.

Duke Edward turned to Keela. "You have made some very serious claims," he said. "What proof do you have?"

For a moment, the thief had no answer—weren't Conor and the amulet enough? Then Keela remembered the hag. "In your chapel lies an old woman," she cried. "She is the midwife who tended Lady Katherine. Baroness Von Drek threw her in the dungeon, but Conor and I rescued her!"

"You there," said the duke, pointing to a guard.

"Go to the chapel and see if the girl speaks the truth."

In a few moments, the guard returned, carrying the hag. The old woman was unconscious, but she was alive. Upon seeing her condition, Duke Edward called for a healer. A woman in white robes stepped out of the crowd. She laid her right hand upon the hag's brow and began to chant softly. The healer's hand began to glow, like an ember from a fire. The hag moaned, and her eyelids fluttered, revealing her empty sockets. The healer stepped away.

"Who are you?" asked the duke.

"Look closer, Duke Edward," replied the hag, "and perhaps you will know me, for I was at your wife's side on the night she died. I was there when she begged me to save her son—your son, who stands before you now."

The duke walked over to Conor. He stared once again at the boy's face.

For a while, no one moved or spoke. Then the hag broke the silence.

"Do you not recognize him?" she asked. "Do you not see the traces of Lady Katherine, your lost love?"

Tears welled in the duke's eyes, and he wrapped his arms around Conor in a warm embrace. He then turned to the crowd. "You came here tonight to meet my heir," said the duke. "I present to you Conor, my son!"

The crowd applauded. All except the baroness, of course. And Rufus. He simply sat in his chair, too dumbfounded to move.

Chapter Ten

The thief kneeled at the edge of the woodland pool, gazing at her own reflection.
Two weeks had passed since she had
last visited this spot—since she had
spied on a handsome shepherd, waiting for her
chance to snare a treasure. It seemed so long ago.
The willows had already begun to turn yellow with
the onset of autumn, dropping their leaves upon the
water's surface. The sad face in the water did not
even look like her own.

"Hey, you!" she called at the face. "No time for
such silliness!" The thief plunged her hand into the

water, destroying the image.

The birthday party for Rufus had come to a spectacular end. Duke Edward had invited the revelers to celebrate until dawn. He was a kind man, and he was grateful to Keela for all she had done to reunite him with Conor. Upon seeing Conor's affection for the thief, he graciously suggested that she remain in the castle as his guest, as long as she chose to do so. He even assigned her three ladies-in-waiting. Then Duke Edward spirited Conor away, so that he and his son could become better acquainted.

Apart from a few glimpses, that was the last Keela had seen of her friend—he was kept too busy by the tutors the duke had assigned to him, as well as by the duke himself. Whenever she tried to see him, Conor's social secretary proclaimed it was "simply impossible," but that Keela should try again the next day.

For three days and nights, the thief slept upon a down-filled bed, wore dresses of the finest fabric, and dined until she almost forgot what it was to know hunger.

Yet, instead of a royal refuge, her new home felt more like a prison. The residents of Durham Castle had readily embraced Conor as their future lord, but they were not nearly as fond of Keela. After all, she was a peasant—and a common thief at that! Such

sentiments were never voiced directly, but Keela
could not help getting the message from their
actions.

The ladies of the castle clutched at their neck-
laces whenever she walked past, as if they were
afraid she would snatch their finery right off their
throats. When seated at a table or a garden bench,
they would smile feebly and nod, but place one hand
over the other to conceal their rings. Although the
castle guards followed her in the pretense of serving
her needs, Keela knew they were watching her
every move, just in case she pocketed a silver
candlestick or some other object of value.

She began to suspect that *any* theft would be
blamed on her—and she wondered how long it
would take before someone intentionally made her a
scapegoat. So she donned her old attire and slipped
away from the castle, vowing never to return.

That vow proved hard to keep. She wanted to see
Conor again. Soon, she had decided, she would
begin a journey. And it didn't seem right not to say
good-bye.

When the thief approached Durham Castle,
night had already fallen, and a full moon lit the sky.
The guards at the gate admitted her, though not
without complaint. Keela went straight toward the
chapel and climbed the tower. She knew better than

to try reaching Conor through his social secretary—especially at night. Soon she was out on the castle wall, edging slowly along a familiar ledge. When she reached the window, she slipped inside as silently as a ghost.

Conor sat at a table, staring into a book. His brow was furrowed with intense concentration. Keela stood in the shadows of the room for a moment, watching him. Already he looked different. His clothing was finely tailored and his golden hair was neatly trimmed. But it was more than that. Just a short time ago, Conor looked like a shepherd, or even a fellow thief. Now, to all appearances, Conor was a noble youth. They were worlds apart.

Suddenly he turned, as if he had felt her gaze upon him.

"Keela!" he exclaimed. He rushed to her side and clasped her hand. "It's so good to see you! Why did you disappear? And how on earth did you get in here?"

"In answer to the second question, I came through the window," said the thief. "As to the first—well, I promised the old woman I'd help you claim your birthright. After that, I had no reason to stay."

Conor's smile faded. "I see," he said, trying to hide his disappointment. "Where have you been?"

A scene from the DRAGON STRIKE™ video

"Here and there," replied the thief. She struggled to sound casual. "You know I'm the wandering type."

"I guess that's true," Conor replied. He started to speak, but stopped, as if he were unsure of what to say next.

"And you?" asked Keela gently. "How is the life of a nobleman?"

Conor smiled. "Not as easy as it once seemed. I spend endless hours with tutors and trainers, studying geography, law, and etiquette. And you'll be pleased to know that I'm finally learning how to fight with a sword."

The thief started to laugh, remembering their battle against the three guards in the village. "That's right—I almost killed you when I threw that blade! But any time there's a tent pole around, I'd still bet on you."

She gazed at the plush chamber around them. "You know, the first time I saw this room, Rufus was here. You're a big improvement."

"Thanks," Conor replied. "Rufus is an odd sort, but he isn't really evil like his mother. Turns out he didn't want to be the duke's heir anyway. Last I heard, he joined that theater troupe."

Keela grinned, imagining what kind of an addition he would make next to Siril and Elbert. "Well, he wasn't exactly the ruling type," she said. "You are, though. Being the son of a duke suits you, Conor."

He didn't answer. Instead, he simply stared at her longingly. Keela felt awkward, and suddenly a little sad. "I heard the old woman from the dungeon is doing fine," she said.

"She's more than fine," Conor replied. "After my father imprisoned the baroness, he sold off some of her holdings and gave the money to the midwife. Now she lives in a comfortable cottage, not far from the pool where we met. You should visit her."

"Maybe I will," said Keela. She paused, then added, "And I guess that's my cue to leave."

Conor touched her on the shoulder and leaned close to her ear. "Why don't you stay, Keela?" he whispered. "We make a good team, don't you think?"

The thief smiled. "I doubt the people of this duchy would agree with you. They'll never accept a thief as their lady. Besides, I'm not cut out for a life of leisure. I've decided to go home."

"I thought this was your home," Conor replied. "I mean, the woods and the pool . . ."

"They have been for a while, but I was raised on King Halvor's lands to the west. Things have changed there, I've heard, though maybe not for the better. Who knows? Maybe I'll even rescue another noble!"

She touched Conor's hand. "Good-bye, Conor, and good luck."

The thief turned and began to climb out the window.

Conor chuckled. "You could use the door, you know!"

"Why start now?" asked Keela. "Besides, I don't have many friends among the castle guards."

The thief began to ease back onto the ledge.

"Stop, thief!" cried Conor softly.

Keela laughed. "What now?"

"*I* haven't said good-bye," Conor answered. He walked to the window and touched Keela's hair, then bent down and kissed her.

When at last he pulled away, Keela winked. "Maybe I'll see you again sometime," she said.

"Stranger things have happened," Conor replied.

The thief dropped onto the ledge and began to make her way across the wall.

Suddenly a guard called out. "Intruder on the wall!"

"Not again," Keela muttered.

Before Conor could shout for his protectors to stop, the guard fired an arrow. The thief dodged, lost her grip, and plunged into the moat . . . again.

Though her recent journeys are mainly flights of fancy, Andria Hayday has clambered through castles, ruins, and mud slicks in a dozen countries. She has covered a broad range of nonfiction topics as a free-lance writer, from health care to highway cave-ins. Currently on staff at TSR, Inc., she has also developed material for the DRAGON STRIKE™ game, as well as for the RAVENLOFT® and AL-QADIM™ fantasy game worlds.

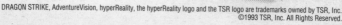

CHARGE Into a World OF MONSTERS Magic AND Treasure!

Imagine you and your friends are the heroes in the time of knights, castles and medieval adventure. You are about to enter a most mysterious dungeon. Navigate its danger-filled corridors. Fight off hordes of vicious monsters. And, if your party survives, find an incredible treasure-trove. Discover The Classic DUNGEON™ Game . . .
the treasure, monsters and magic of your imagination are waiting!
On sale now at book, game, and hobby stores everywhere!

TSR #1045 IBSN #0-88038-733-5
Sug. Retail $19.95; CAN $25.50; £11.99 U.K.
Incl. VAT

When she gets home, Wale hasn't called back or left a message on her phone. The least he can do and he hasn't even done that. Why would she expect more from him? She eats dinner and still no phone call from him.

Tonight she watches a Hollywood film that takes place during a genocide in an imaginary African country. The usual elements are in the film: the benevolent missionary priest; the hopeful expatriate and cynical foreign journalist who has a change of conscience; the sidekick African intellectual and the corrupt local politician. Red-eyed African military men drive around in trucks brandishing machine guns. Arrogant UN troops are unsympathetic to the hungry refugees and barefoot children. The children run after their trucks. A token pet dog gets slaughtered. There is much drumming and singing and panoramic shots of green hills. Normally, she allows herself to be seduced, but not today. It is painful to watch, almost as if a mass sacrifice has taken place so the journalist and the expatriate can fall in love.

She has never recognized this Africa. She is increasingly dissatisfied with what she sees on television about Africa, most especially on the news. Not the barrage of news clips on wars and poverty-stricken villages—after all, they are not made up—but the lack of perspective and continued absence of her experiences.

What she would give to see a boring old banker going on about capital growth, as they do in Nigeria, just for once. Why not? Don't they exist? Don't they count? Or are they so well assimilated into the rest of the world that they are no longer visible? Or—and this would be a conspiracy of the most tragic consequence—are Westerners, now that Africans readily process themselves for Western consumption, developing a preference for Africans who are pure and unadulterated?

Morning sickness is meant to prepare her womb for her child. She is beginning to believe it is also preparing her as well because it is becoming more and more trying to get up and eat breakfast, yet she does. She has to get enough nutrients and stay active. She thinks of her growing child as a friend, a friend she is getting acquainted with. She must have grown up to some extent because she is able to put her fears aside, and what might have been a sense of failure is now a determination to be worthy of being a mother.